The Adventures of

ELI

and

TIG

ISBN 978-1-63874-587-7 (paperback)
ISBN 978-1-63874-588-4 (digital)

Christian Faith Publishing, Inc.
832 Park Avenue
Meadville, PA 16335
www.christianfaithpublishing.com

Printed in the United States of America.

The Adventures of

ELI

and

TIG

ALORA JOHNS

Chapter 1

In the state of Kentucky, in the town of Georgetown, there lived a boy named Eli. He had a big family. His mother was beautiful, was a fabulous cook, and sang so very sweetly. His father was handsome and strong and took care of the family. He had a pretty sister who loved all things shiny and glittery. He had four brothers; two were older and two were younger. They had so much fun together most of the time. *But* his best friend was Tig!

Now you may not think it strange for a boy to have a friend that is not his brother or some other boy, but you see, Tig is a *pig*!

"A pig!" you say. "How can this be?"

This is the thing you must know. Tig is no ordinary pig!

"What!" you say. "How can a pig be anything other than an ordinary pig?"

Let me tell just how it is. Here are a few things to know about this oh so very special pig.

First, Tig is smart!

"But," you may say, "most pigs are smart."

Ahh! But you see, Tig is human-smart plus pig-smart!

Second, Tig is fast!

"But," you may say, "most pigs are fast."

That is true, but Tig is human-fast and pig-fast.

Third, Tig is clean.

"Clean!" you say. "No way! Most pigs are *not* clean! Most pigs are dirty. They are even muddy!"

But Tig is clean and tidy. Tidier than most little boys!

Fourth, Tig walks on his back legs.

"What! *No! No!*" you say. "Now you are going too far! Pigs do not walk on their back legs! This I know for sure!"

But you see, Tig is no ordinary pig! He does, indeed, walk on his hind legs. He even runs on them! Calm yourself now as I go on to tell you more about Tig.

Fifth, Tig wears clothes. He wears T-shirts and shorts and sneakers and socks! Sometimes he even wears a baseball cap!

"Are there more unbelievable things about Tig? Smart, clean, walks on his hind legs, wears clothes!" you say. "Next you will be telling me he talks!"

Sixth, why yes. How did you know? Tig does talk! He reads, and he imagines wonderful things. He can even do math! He knows many things and can think up lots of fun adventures. Such a special pig, that Tig!

Oh, I almost forgot. Tig is funny too! Now sit back, and let me tell you about all the wonderful adventures Eli and Tig have together. Just sit back and relax. You will enjoy hearing all these stories about Eli and his friend, Tig. Pretty soon you will be wanting to have a friend like Tig!

Chapter 2

This is the story of how Eli met Tig.

One day, Eli was bored! He had read all his books, made his bed, picked up his stuff, helped his mom do chores, and now, he couldn't find anything he wanted to play! His father was at work, his mother was cooking, his sister was in her room doing what girls do, and all his brothers were busy doing things without him. What a bummer! He let out a big sigh!

His mom looked at him and said, "Eli, it is nice outside. Why don't you ride your bike around the block and get some fresh air? When you get back from your ride, I will play with you."

Eli got out his bike and started around the block. No one was out! Not a single kid. Not even an adult! No cats and no dogs were to be seen. He kept riding and thinking that he was tired of being alone. He wanted someone to play with. He was not very picky about who it was. It would just be fun to play with any old someone.

Just then, he saw the strangest sight! At first, he thought he saw a little boy standing by the sidewalk. The closer he got, he saw that it was the strangest-looking kid he had ever seen. He shook his head to clear his eyes because this kid looked just like a pig!

Man, that is sad to look like a pig! Eli thought. *I will smile and be nice to him. I like pigs, but I wouldn't want to look like one!*

In fact, Eli really liked pigs. He had stuffed pigs, a piggy bank, a pig blanket, pig games, a pig shirt—yes, Eli liked pigs, but he still did not want to look like one. Eli slowed his bike and smiled at the weird kid. The kid smiled back and waved to Eli. Eli waved back. He stopped to say hi to the strange kid. Then the kid started talking so fast; Eli couldn't keep up with him.

"Whoa! Whoa! Slow down," said Eli. "Say all that again only slower this time."

"Hi, Eli, my name is Tig. I have been waiting for you to come for a long time! I thought you might not come today. We are going to have so much fun together! I can hardly wait to start! I am so excited!"

"You know me?" asked Eli.

"Know you? Of course I do. I am your BFF. Best friend forever! Don't you want someone to have fun with? Sure, you do! Somebody goofed and forgot to tell you, but that is all right because you are here now! We can get started!"

"Started with what?" asked Eli.

"Our grand adventure, of course," answered Tig.

Eli got off his bike and took a long look at Tig. He was shorter than Eli. He was rounder than Eli.

This kid may be standing up and wearing clothes, but he really is a pig! thought Eli.

Just then, Tig said, "Of course I am a pig. That is what you ordered. I was so happy someone wanted a pig for a friend, so here I am!"

"Ordered? Pig? Friend? You heard my thoughts?"

"Well, of course I did. Where do you think I come from but from your thoughts!" said Tig. "Come on! Time is wasting. Follow me!" And off Tig went behind the bushes.

Eli looked around for a minute and thought, *This could be interesting!*

Then he followed Tig behind the bushes and discovered a whole other world. A world he had never known.

Chapter 3

The adventure began.

Eli stopped short when he got on the other side of those bushes. He had never seen anything like what he was looking at right now! He stood right there, eyes bugged out and mouth wide open, staring at the scene in front of him. Everything was different and weird and wonderful and topsy-turvy! He could not decide what to look at first. There were so many strange things to look at! Everything was bright and colorful and happy and very busy! Not to mention crazy! He started laughing and laughing as hard as he could until he finally fell down!

When he caught his breath, he looked up at Tig and asked him, "Where is this place and how did we get here?"

"What?" said Tig. "Don't you recognize it? This is your imagination. It is all the stuff stored up in your head. All the things you have imagined are right here in front of you!"

"Where did it come from? This imagination you say I have?" asked Eli.

"Where all the good stuff comes from, Eli," said Tig. "It is a gift from God for you to explore and have fun with! So come on. Let's get started!"

Where to start? What to pick? Which one first?

Finally Tig, getting impatient, pointed to a little tree to one side. It was a small tree, and it was covered with little egg-like shapes. Each shape was blinking different colors. They were whirling or bouncing up and down. Some were humming, ringing, or beeping!

"Pick one!" Tig said. "Inside will be our first adventure."

Eli looked at Tig. Then he looked at the tree again and grinned. He was ready for adventure. He was excited to be able to tell his brothers about it all, but first, he had to pick his adventure! He reached out his hand to grab one, but before he could pick one, a flashing orange beeping egg jumped into his hand.

Looking surprised, he heard Tig laugh and say, "Looks like your adventure picked you! Open it up and we can go!"

Eli carefully started opening the little egg shape when an orange cloud came out of the egg and surrounded both him and Tig. When the cloud disappeared, Eli found himself on the pitcher's mound right in the middle of a baseball game. But this was no ordinary baseball game! All the players were animals dressed in their team uniforms.

Eli looked down and saw he was in a baseball uniform too! And so was Tig! He looked questioningly at Tig, but Tig was talking with a zebra who was wearing a different uniform. Both Tig and the zebra's shirt had *Coach* written on the back!

Tig walked over to Eli and told him they were on the *Friendly Farm* team, and their opponents were the *Zany Zoo* team. Eli was the pitcher. It was up to him to strike out the Zoo team so they could get up to bat.

Eli looked around at the players in the outfield. They were all looking at him and giving a thumbs-up or something close to it—a paw up, a wing up, a hoof up—you get the idea. Then he looked at the Zoo dugout, and he saw all these eyes staring at him. Challenging him! They looked scary! Eli wasn't sure it was a good idea to be playing with those guys.

Wow! He looked at Tig, who just smiled and said, "Don't worry! They can't bite, eat, or stomp on you. It is against the rules!"

Eli took a deep breath as the umpire, Bob Baboon, yelled, "Play ball! Batter up!"

This was going to be a very interesting game, thought Eli. He was not sure if all the rules were the same as the rules he knew, but he liked the "no biting, no eating, or no stomping on" rules! He turned to face the first batter. They were in the top of the eighth inning, and the score was tied 6 all! The team lineups looked like this:

<table>
<tr><td>*Friendly Farm Team*</td><td>*Zany Zoo Team*</td></tr>
<tr><td>Pitcher: Eli</td><td>Pitcher: Lenny Lemur</td></tr>
<tr><td>Catcher: Toro Bull</td><td>Relief Pitcher: Charlie Chimp</td></tr>
<tr><td>First Base: Red Rooster</td><td>Catcher: Gary Gorilla</td></tr>
<tr><td>Second Base: Richie Ram</td><td>First Base: Griz Bear</td></tr>
<tr><td>Third Base: Jack Dog</td><td>Second Base: Leo Lion</td></tr>
<tr><td>Shortstop: Billy Goat</td><td>Third Base: Harry Hippo</td></tr>
<tr><td>Center Field: Max Mule</td><td>Shortstop: Reggie Rhino</td></tr>
<tr><td>Right Field: Grady Goose</td><td>Center Field: Wally W. Buffalo</td></tr>
<tr><td>Left Field: Buck Stallion</td><td>Right Field: Jerry Giraffe</td></tr>
<tr><td>Coach: Tig Pig</td><td>Left Field: Milton Monkey</td></tr>
<tr><td>Umpires: Bob and Bill Baboon</td><td>Coach: Zip Zebra</td></tr>
</table>

The Friendly Farm Team

Red Rooster

ELi

Tig Pig

Grady Goose

Richie RAm

Max Mule

Billy Goat

Toro Bull

Jack Dog

Buck Stal...

18

The Zany Zoo Team

Wally W. Buffalo

Charlie Chimp

Zip Zebra

Milton Monkey

Lenny Lemur

Gary Gorilla

Harry Hippo

Reggie Rhino

Jerry Giraffe

Leo Lion

Griz Bear

The Friendly Farm team uniforms were striped green and white. Zany Zoo uniforms were rainbow-striped.

Very quickly, Eli looked around and checked the field. At home plate was the catcher, Toro Bull, who quickly gave him a hoof up. Up at bat was Griz Bear. His beady eyes stared down Eli, daring him to pitch. At first base ready for action was Red Rooster, with his feathers all ruffled up!

Well, it is time to play ball, thought Eli. He turned to home plate, wound up, and threw a fastball right over center plate.

The ump yelled, "Strike!"

Griz let out a loud roar of displeasure, but it would not be his last. Eli continued to throw strikes and balls until Griz struck out and had to return to the dugout. He growled his displeasure the whole way back!

The Farm team crowd roared with excitement. Two more strikeouts, and they would be up to bat. You could hear the excitement on each side. One side mooing, baaing, clucking, and honking their excitement, the other side growling and snorting their displeasure. Eli hoped the no biting and eating rule applied to the fans as well as the players.

As the inning progressed, Leo Lion hit a single and was on first base. Harry Hippo struck out for the second out. Just one more to go! Could Eli keep up the pace in the middle of all the strange noises?

Up to bat came Lenny Lemur. The crowd quieted. Lenny was the best hitter in the whole league. He always hit a home run. Everyone held their breath. Eli looked at Toro, who sent him the signal to pitch a long low curveball. Eli wasn't sure what to do. He wanted to pitch a fastball down the center of the plate, but he knew he should trust his catcher. So very carefully, he threw his best long low curveball! Lenny swung!

"*Strike one!*" called the ump.

Screeching and jumping up and down, Lenny was ticked off. Bob, the ump, threatened to throw him out of the game if he did not calm down. Lenny turned to the plate with steely concentration. Bouncing his bat on his shoulder, he stared at Eli. Eli stared back. He threw outside.

"Ball!" the ump called.

Lenny sneered at Eli. Eli looked around. Tig was jumping up and down, grinning at him. Toro gave him the signal for a low pitch to the edge of plate. With total concentration, Eli threw the ball. Lenny swung and missed.

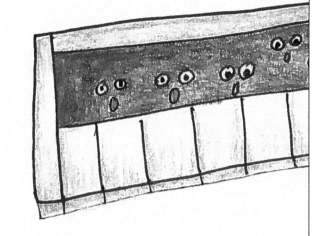

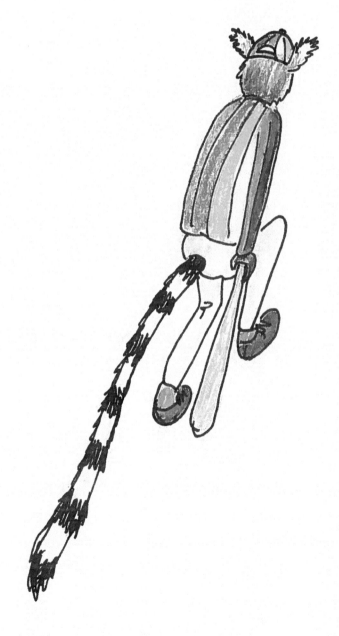

"*Strike two*!" yelled the ump.

Two strikes on Lenny! This had never happened before! The crowd was silent. You could feel the tension in the air. Could Eli really strike out Lenny Lemur? All eyes were on the field. Everyone took a deep breath as they watched. No one even blinked! Eli reared back and threw his best fastball right over the center of the plate. It went so fast Lenny didn't even get a chance to swing!

"*Strike three! You are out*!" called Bob the Ump.

A gasp came out of the stands. No one could believe their eyes! Lenny had struck out! The whole ballpark was silent! Then it erupted into shouting and joy and moaning and outrage, depending on which team you supported.

Finally, after things calmed down, Lenny, with his head held low, headed back to the dugout. A tear rolled down his face. All his teammates were sad for him. But in the Farm Team dugout, there was laughing and shouting and high fives, or close to it, and chest bumps. What excitement! Maybe they could win this game!

ZANY ZOO

Umps - Bill + Bob Baboon

27

In the Zoo dugout, it was very quiet. In the corner, plans were being made for a comeback. The Zoo players eyed the other team and plotted and schemed how to defeat the Farm team. The Zany Zoo team had been known to play fast and loose with the rules. What could they be plotting to do so they can win? Would they play fair, or would they do something sneaky? From the looks of things in their dugout, I would bet on something sneaky.

Meanwhile, in the Farm team dugout, the team was jubilant. All was excitement and joy as they were quite unaware of the other team's plots. The Farm team got their batting lineup set. The Zoo team went out to the field as the ump called for play to resume.

First up to bat was Richie Ram. Richie is a good hitter and can be depended on to get a base hit or a double. Lenny Lemur stared at Richie, determined to strike him out. *Whish!* A fastball tore past Richie, and he swung. Strike 1. *Whish!* Another fastball. Strike 2. Everyone was on the edge of their seat as catcher Gary Gorilla signaled to Lenny to throw a low curveball. But Lenny was still upset about striking out and didn't pay attention to Gary's signal. He threw another fastball right down the center! This time, Richie was ready. Crack! He hit that ball straight out to center field, past Wally W. Buffalo, and hit the fence. Wally ran to get the ball, but Richie had made it to second base before he got it and threw the ball in. Richie was on second base and second baseman Leo Lion was breathing down his neck. The tension was rising, as was Lenny's temper, which is known to be hot and furious! Up next to bat was Red Rooster. Now Red is a great first baseman, but when batting, he can get his feathers all ruffled and not concentrate. But today, Red had a steely look in his beady little eyes, which was new. He was determined not to let his team down. He stared out at Lenny. Lenny stared back at Red. Then the ball came flying at Red, hitting him right in the head! *Bonk!* Red staggered for a moment. Lenny looked wide-eyed! He had never hit a batter before! Today was not Lenny's day. Bob the Ump sent Lenny to the dugout and Red to first base. Dazed but okay, Red happily ran/flew to first base.

Chapter 4

The Zoo team put in their substitute pitcher, Charlie Chimp. Now Charlie was a good pitcher when he is not distracted, but he was almost always distracted.

Coach Zip Zebra came out to the pitcher's mound to make sure Charlie was focused. Now with two men on base and Toro Bull up to bat, all eyes were on the field. Gary the Catcher grunted! Toro snorted! Charlie Chimp scratched his butt and grinned. Then Charlie stood up tall, wound up, and threw a screwball. It went up. It went down. It went in circles. It looped and looped until it finally straightened out and flew straight over the plate! Strike 1! Toro looked dazed. Then before you knew it, another ball came zooming over the plate for strike 2! Oh no! What is happening? Charlie wound up and threw the curviest curveball ever thrown for strike 3! Toro struck out! With head held low, Toro walked slowly back to the dugout.

Next up was Jack Dog. Jack was very excitable and was barking and yipping all the way to the plate. Very quickly—in fact, so quickly most everyone missed it—Jack struck out! How can this be?

Slowly, right fielder Grady Goose waddled up to bat. Grady was a little slow in the running department, but he was a good hitter. Charlie looked at Grady, did a back flip, and threw a zinger of a pitch right over the plate for strike 1. Grady ruffled his gray feathers and grabbed his bat tighter. Then when Charlie threw another pitch, Grady stretched out his wings and hit it right down the baseline so hard it sped past Griz at first base. Grady made it to first base before the ball was thrown back in. Now the bases were loaded. Grady on first, Red on second, and Richie on third! The tension in the stands was high. You could feel the excitement! This was the most thrilling game the fans had ever seen. No one wanted to miss a thing. Who was up to bat next? Could they hit a homer and get ahead? Maybe they could win the game? Or would they strike out?

Tig turned to Eli and said, "Eli, you're up."

What! You've got to be kidding! thought Eli. He looked around at his teammates and saw their encouraging faces. He knew he could not let his team down. He shook himself, pulled his shoulders back, picked up a bat, and walked out to home plate. He could feel the hot breath of Gary Gorilla on his back. He felt every eye from the Zoo dugout staring daggers at him. Taking a deep breath, he took his stance and looked out at Charlie. Charlie was flipping around like a goofball. He was having a great time.

Finally, the ump called, "Play ball!"

Charlie stopped flipping and flung a fastball right past Eli's nose. Ball 1! Staring straight at Charlie, Eli could see Charlie was trying to be serious. He wound up to pitch, but just as he was letting go of the ball, a butterfly flitted past Charlie. He let the ball fall from his hand and roll toward home plate as he chased after the butterfly! Ball 2! What is going on? Eli wanted to hit the ball so they could get ahead, but Charlie was being a silly chimp! Coach Zip was yelling at Charlie from the dugout. But Charlie was more interested in the butterfly that had perched on his nose than listening to the coach. Finally, the butterfly flew off, and Charlie heard Coach Zip. He shrugged his shoulders and threw a fast curveball right over home plate!

"Strike one, ball two!" called the ump.

Now Eli was worried. What was that nutty Chimp going to do next? Charlie was lying on his back picking his toenails when suddenly he picked up the ball with one of his feet and flung it toward Eli. It went up! It went down! It spun around and then sped over the plate for strike 2.

"Really? A strike? He wasn't even standing up!" Eli looked around for someone to object, but no one did! Apparently, this was normal for this ball league! Turning toward the pitcher, Eli saw that Charlie was getting ready to throw the ball again! Charlie was spinning and jumping and flipping when quick as a wink, he let go of a throw that went straight up in the air, curved around, and headed for home plate. Whoosh! Ball 3! The count is three balls and two strikes.

Eli's head is spinning! Taking a deep gulp of air, he steadies himself for whatever comes next from that crazy chimp.

"Steady, steady," he said to himself, "you have this."

Just then, the ball went sailing across the base. Eli swung and hit. The ball went flying up, up, up and over the fence! *Home run*! He made a home run! There was much hooting and hollering as the players made their way around the bases one by one to score! Hurrah! The Farm Team was four points ahead!

The happier the Farm team became, the angrier the Zoo team became. As the Farm team was celebrating, the Zoo team was grumbling and growling something about putting plan "Underbelly" to work!

At last, the umps got everyone back playing ball. The rest of the inning was tame. Buck Stallion made a single, and then Billy Goat was struck out by a crazy "should have been illegal but wasn't" pitch. The end of the eighth inning, and the Farm team was ahead by four points.

All too soon, the teams had switched places, and Eli found himself back on the pitcher's mound. He looked around. Everyone was in their place. It was beginning to look normal to see a bull as catcher and a rooster as first base and a gorilla at bat. Eli was feeling good about his team. Then he looked at the Zoo dugout. If there was ever a time to be afraid, it would be now! He had never seen so many angry eyes staring at him. Eli just looked back at his team's faces and knew it was all good.

First up to bat was Gary Gorilla. Gosh! He was a big guy! Eli knew if Gary ever hit the ball, it would go over the fence. He looked to Toro, who just shrugged as if to say, "Nothing we can do with him."

But Eli had a plan. He would walk Gary, then strike out the next three players.

Some plan! he thought. *Hope it works*.

Eli threw a wild high pitch. Ball 1. Then he threw a low ground ball for ball 2. At the base, Gary was catching on to Eli's plan, and he was not happy about it. Very carefully, Eli threw the next ball wide off the plate, but he had not figured on Gary's long gorilla arms. Gary just reached over the plate and hit that ball. It was a bouncing ground ball right between second and third base.

Billy Goat tried his best to catch it, but just as he got there, it bounced sideways. Billy missed the ball. Jack Dog finally caught it, but by then, Gary was firmly on first base. Red was jumping up and down flapping his wings. He was trying his best not to get squashed by Gary! Gary took up a lot of room! Murmurs of approval came from the Zoo dug out. Something seemed funny to Eli. Eli looked around with a puzzled look on his face. He was positive there were too many players in the Zoo dugout. But when he looked again, things looked normal.

Huh? he thought, *this is weirder than the normal weird around here.*

Up next in the rotation was Jerry Giraffe. Jerry was a little awkward and slow. He always swung after the ball passed him. He was an easy out! Milton Monkey popped up at home base next. If Eli thought the chimp was crazy, this monkey made Charlie look calm! Milton was bouncing around so much; Eli was not sure where to throw. Finally, he just threw a ball hoping it would be in the right spot! But it wasn't! Milton Monkey hit that ball all the way into the outfield! He scampered to first base. Gary ambled to second!

What just happened? Eli thought. There was a chance they could lose their lead. When he looked at home base, there stood Reggie in all his rhino armor. Eli looked for Tig. That pig was nowhere to be found! Then he looked at Toro. Toro just smiled and nodded to Eli to throw his fastball. Sure enough, while Reggie was powerful, he was not fast. Three fastballs later, Reggie was out!

"Whew!" Eli breathed a sigh of relief.

Two outs down. One to go. We were almost done. Eli felt something behind him staring. He turned slowly to look. There in the shadows, he saw three pairs of red eyes attached to three dark-hunched shadows! He heard a low evil-sounding laugh. He turned to look at his teammates, but they were all staring with fear at those same eyes! What in the world was it?

Suddenly, the three shapes bolted out of the shadows onto the field, knocking over and biting Grady Goose, sending feathers flying everywhere. The three shapes separated and ran for Red Rooster and Jack Dog.

Just when it looked like all was lost, Toro bellowed at the top of his bull voice, "Hyenas! Run!"

45

Lowering his head, Toro chased after the hyenas. His horns flashing in the sunlight! Billy Goat and Richie Ram lowered their heads and joined the chase. The dust flew, horns flashed, teeth gnashed. There was growling and grunting! Confusion was everywhere! Soon (but it seemed a lot longer) all was quiet. The hyenas and their evil laughter were gone. They had run away thoroughly beaten. Toro Bull stood proudly in the center of the diamond, making sure they did not return.

When the shock wore off, everyone looked around to see if anyone was hurt. Billy Goat lost some of his whiskers, but he said he needed a shave anyway. Richie Ram was protected from the hyenas's bites by his thick wooly fleece. He just needed a bath. It was time for his weekly bath, so it was not a big deal. Grady Goose looked the worse. Everyone looked to see how he was.

Standing strong with his head held high, he said bravely, "I lost some feathers, and I am sore where they were pulled out, but they will grow back in time."

A big sigh of relief went around the field! Everyone was okay. They all thanked Toro, Richie, and Billy. They were heroes that day! They were brave and had defended their friends from harm.

Chapter 5

When everything had settled down, Eli noticed that the Zoo team was gone. Not one of them was in the dugout except for Coach Zip Zebra. He looked strange because he was not black and white all over but black, white, and red. He was embarrassed and ashamed of his team. Tig asked Zip Zebra why he was embarrassed. Then the whole story came out.

It seemed some of the Zoo players wanted to get the game canceled because they thought they would lose. They came up with this plan called "Underbelly." They arranged to have some hoodlum hyenas scare the Farm team members away, so the game would be canceled. They never wanted anyone to get hurt. They just did not want to lose! But you see, hyenas never play nice! You cannot trust them to keep their word. When you play with those who do not treat others kindly, you usually get in a mess!

When the Zoo players saw the mess they had created, they slunk away in shame. They left Zip to try and clean up their mess! Poor Zip! He had nothing to do with the plan, and yet, he was standing up, taking the blame for his team. Zip stood there with his face red, and his head hung in shame!

The whole Farm Team and the umpires got in a huddle to decide what to do. After some discussion and debate, they made a decision. Umps Bob and Bill Baboon stepped forward.

"Zip," they said, "we have all voted to forgive you and your team. But since you were behind in the last inning of the game and the game was stopped because of what your team did, we are calling this game as a win for the Friendly Farm team. Tig Pig wants to say something to you and your whole team."

Tig stepped forward and in a loud voice said, "Zip, we don't want any hard feelings over this. We want to invite you and your whole team to an after-the-game party. Just one thing—*no hyenas*!"

As Tig was speaking, the whole Zoo team had slowly come onto the ball field. They were all looking sheepish, which is strange to see on wild animals. But Tig was not surprised to see them. He knew they were not far off. That was why he was talking so loudly. After a round of apologies from the Zoo team, the party started. They played music and sang and ate food and laughed 'till they couldn't laugh anymore. They partied until it was time to go home.

Eli looked around at his new friends and smiled! He would have a lot to tell his family, especially his brothers. Next time, maybe he would invite them to come on an adventure with him. Not *the* END but just the beginning of many more exciting adventures with Eli and Tig.

About the Author

Alora Johns is an artist and teacher. Her first love is art, whether it is painting, drawing, or doodling. She enjoys kids and loves to help them enter the wonderful world of creating art by freeing them to explore their imagination! What wonderful journeys she has gone on with her students! In this book, she invites you to go on one such adventure.